THE SANTA CLAUSE

A Novel by DAPHNE SKINNER
Based on the Motion Picture from WALT DISNEY PICTURES
In association with HOLLYWOOD PICTURES
Executive Producers RICHARD BAKER RICK MESSINA JAMES MILLER
Based on the Screenplay Written by LEO BENVENUTI & STEVE RUDNICK
Produced by BRIAN REILLY JEFFREY SILVER ROBERT NEWMYER
Directed by JOHN PASQUIN

HYPERION PAPERBACKS FOR CHILDREN
NEW YORK

Text © 1994 by Hyperion Books for Children.
Story, art, and photographs © THE WALT DISNEY COMPANY.
All rights reserved.
Printed in the United States of America.
For information address
Hyperion Books for Children, 114 Fifth Avenue,
New York, New York 10011.
SCHOOL BOOK CLUB EDITION

ISBN: 0-7868-1058-0
Library of Congress Catalog Card Number: 94-78141

Chapter One

Charlie Calvin slumped in the backseat of his mother's car. As usual, they were parked outside his father's house, waiting, because, as usual, his dad was late. I just hope I can leave early, thought Charlie. It was hard enough spending weekends with Dad, but Christmas Eve? The worst. Charlie glanced at the single string of Christmas lights over Dad's front door. Typical. Every other house on the street was aglow with bright, blinking holiday decorations; angels, reindeer, even flamingos wearing Santa hats. But not Dad's house. One pathetic string of lights. And they were falling down.

Charlie sighed. His father definitely didn't have it together.

At last another car pulled up behind them. Scott Calvin got out and gave them a cheery wave. With a sigh, Charlie waved back halfheartedly and followed his mother out of the car.

"Laura! Charlie! Come in!" said Scott when they reached the porch. "Hey, Sport, why don't you go look under the tree? There might be some things there for you."

Charlie was glad to get away before his dad and his mom started bickering. He knew it was only a matter of time. But he could hardly believe what he found in the living room. A little fake tree with spindly blue branches. Under it, three lumpy packages wrapped in brown paper. Pathetic.

"So, what do you think, Sport?" his father asked when Charlie came back into the hallway.

Charlie tried not to sound too disappointed. "There aren't that many presents there," he mumbled.

"Well, Santa hasn't come yet," said Scott.

"Neal doesn't believe in Santa," said Charlie. Neal was his mom's new husband.

"Well, Neal's head comes to a point," Scott snapped. He couldn't stand Neal.

"He's a doctor," said Charlie. Personally, he thought Neal was cool.

Scott snorted. "He isn't a doctor, Sport. He's a psychiatrist."

Just then a horn honked outside. Neal.

Scott turned to his ex-wife angrily. "Did that jerk tell Charlie there was no Santa?" he whispered.

"He only said that Santa Claus was more like a state of mind than a real person," Charlie's mother answered.

"Kind of like Neal," said Scott.

"We try to give Charlie a firm grasp on reality," Laura replied, a little too loudly.

"Now that's a good idea," answered Scott, raising his voice, too. "We wouldn't want our kid running around using his imagination, now, would we?"

Charlie could feel his stomach knotting up. "Why do you guys always have to fight?" he asked unhappily.

"We're not fighting, Sport," said Scott. "We're arguing. You see, Mom and Neal don't believe in Santa Claus because they've been naughty." A wicked gleam came into his eyes. "They're going to get a lump of coal in their stockings."

"I don't know," said Charlie. "Seems kind of babyish to believe in that stuff."

"Babyish!" exclaimed Scott. "I believe in Santa, and I'm not a baby."

The horn honked again. "You better go," Scott said to Laura. "We wouldn't want to keep Doctor Brilliant waiting."

Charlie and his mom hugged. "I'll see you tomorrow," she whispered.

"Do I have to stay?" Charlie whispered back. He wished he could leave with her. "Will you pick me up tomorrow?"

"Of course I will."

"Early?"

"You'll be fine," she promised.

Charlie wasn't so sure.

❅   ❅   ❅

A few hours later Charlie was even less sure. First his father burned the turkey so badly it looked like a flame-broiled meteorite. Then they had to drive around for ages searching for a place to eat. Charlie didn't know which was harder—finding an open restaurant on Christmas Eve or trying to talk to his dad.

His first big mistake was mentioning Neal. "You know, Neal's a really good cook," he said.

"Yeah, and he does his own dental work," snapped Scott.

"You don't like him much, do you, Dad?" asked Charlie.

Scott's tone of voice softened a little. "Oh, he's okay," he said. "There's just something about the guy that makes me want to . . ."

". . . lash out irrationally?" said Charlie.

Scott looked at him. "Where'd you hear that?"

"From Neal. I learn a lot from him," said Charlie. "He listens to me."

"Yeah, but then he charges you for it," said Scott, pulling up to a restaurant. It was closed. "I listen," he said. "Don't I?"

Charlie just looked at him. Scott pulled away from the restaurant. "You know, Charlie," he said, "you could learn stuff from me, too, if you came to visit more than just every other weekend."

Charlie didn't say anything. What was there to say?

"We'd have a great time," Scott said.

Charlie decided to set his father straight. "We never have a great time," he said flatly.

"How can you say that? Didn't I take you to the Bears game last weekend? That was fun!"

"No, it wasn't," said Charlie. "I don't even like football. I like soccer."

"Soccer!" Scott said, as if it were a life-threatening disease. "It's not even American! Only wimps play soccer."

"I joined a team last month," Charlie told him.

"You did?" said Scott. "I didn't know that."

That's because you don't want to know, thought Charlie.

Scott parked the car in front of a family-style restaurant. "It's open!" he crowed. "We're in luck!"

Charlie winced. "I don't want to eat here," he told his father.

"C'mon," said Scott in an extra-jolly voice. "Everybody likes this."

"Disaster," Charlie muttered as they walked inside. Naturally, his dad didn't even hear him.

❅　　❅　　❅

After dinner they drove home in silence. Charlie changed into his pajamas and climbed into bed, relieved that the evening was almost over. Then Scott announced he was going to read aloud.

"A story?" asked Charlie, surprised. His father never read to him.

"A poem," said Scott. He started reading an old poem that began: "'Twas the night before Christmas . . ." It made Charlie drowsy, and his eyes closed. As they did, his father read, "When out on the lawn there arose such a clatter, I sprang from my bed to see what was the matter. . . ."

Charlie's eyes opened. "What's that?" he asked.

"What's what?"

"*A rose suchak ladder*," said Charlie. "What is it?"

Scott smiled. "Not a *ladder*," he said. "A *clatter*. A big noise. It means, 'there came a big noise.'" He stroked Charlie's forehead. "Time for you to go to sleep, Sport," he said.

But Charlie had a few questions. "How do reindeer fly?" he asked. "They don't have any wings. And if Santa's so fat, how can he get down the chimneys? Besides, what about the people who don't have fireplaces? How does he get into their houses?"

"Look, Sport," said Scott, "believing in something means you just believe in it. Reindeer fly because that's how Santa gets around. You can't stop believing in things just because they don't make any sense."

This was a new idea to Charlie. "So, Dad," he said, "you really *do* believe in Santa?"

"Yeah, Sport," said his father. "I do."

Charlie's eyes fell shut. "Then we'd better leave some cookies and milk for him," he said sleepily. "Just in case . . ."

Scott grinned. "Now you're talking," he said. He felt better than he had all day.

Chapter Two

Later that night, the only sounds in the house were the hum of the refrigerator and the rumble of Scott's snoring. Charlie was fast asleep—until a loud thump from the roof woke him. He lay in bed listening. There it was again. Charlie got out of bed and found his way to Scott's room.

"Dad?" he said, shaking his father awake.

"What is it?" Scott asked, his voice somewhere between a croak and a yawn. His eyes stayed closed.

"I heard a clatter." The thumping noise came again. "There!" Charlie said. "Don't you hear it? A clatter. A big noise. Coming from outside. Dad! I'm scared!"

"It's nothing," snuffled Scott, turning over. "Probably just the wind. Go back to sleep."

Then the noise came again. This time it sounded as if half a dozen heavy barrels were dropping onto the roof. The house shook. Scott's eyes flew open, and he jumped out of bed.

He motioned to Charlie to be quiet. The ceiling creaked. They looked at each other.

"Maybe it's Santa," said Charlie.

"Not now, Charlie," said Scott. He headed for the door.

"You wait here," he said, "and if you hear anything funny, dial nine-one-one, okay?"

Charlie nodded. He listened to his father walk downstairs and onto the back porch. For a moment there was total quiet. Then he heard his father shout, "Hey, you!"

Charlie heard a slithering noise from the roof, followed by a soft thud. He ran downstairs and outside.

The moon hung in the sky like a big white candy wafer, casting deep shadows around the house. Charlie saw his father standing next to a large, dark shape on the ground. Charlie drew closer. The shape was a man.

"Stay back, Charlie," warned Scott. He pushed the man gently with his foot. There was no response—the man lay perfectly still. Grunting with effort, Scott slowly turned him over. Charlie saw with a shock that the man, who had a full white beard and a belly the size of a beach ball, was dressed in a Santa Claus suit. His red cap had slipped off his head, revealing silky white hair. He had bushy white eyebrows, and his round face wore a look of surprise.

"It *is* Santa, Dad!" cried Charlie. And then it hit him. "You killed him!"

Scott winced. "I did not," he said. "And he is not Santa Claus. This is a guy who was trying to break into our house. He fell off the roof."

Charlie wasn't convinced. "He looks like Santa."

"He's got to have some ID on him," said Scott, reaching into the man's pockets. The wallet he found had a business card in it. He and Charlie read it together: "If something should happen to me, put on my suit. The reindeer will know what to do."

10

Scott and Charlie looked at each other. Then they looked up at the roof. A large sleigh harnessed with eight reindeer stood next to their chimney. When they looked down again, the man had vanished. Only the Santa suit remained.

Charlie jumped up and down with excitement. "You gonna put on the suit, Dad? Are you? Are you? Come on, Dad," he demanded, "put it on. 'Cause I wanna go, too!"

"Stop that, Charlie!" said Scott. "We are not going anywhere!"

An all-too-familiar feeling of disappointment made Charlie's voice bitter. "See?" he said. "That's what I was talking about before. You never listen. Every time I want to do something, it's silly. You never do what I want to do. It's always what *you* want to do."

Scott wondered if Charlie was right. He was so confused, he didn't know what to think. He started to pace back and forth. "Okay," he muttered to himself, "reindeer on the roof. Santa suit on the lawn. The guy fell. Not my fault. Still, reindeer on the roof. Hard to explain. Very hard . . ." As he paced, he bumped into a ladder propped up against the side of the house—a ladder he had never seen before.

Charlie rushed over to examine it. "Look here, Dad," he said. "Like the poem."

A metal plaque on the ladder read, The Rose Suchak Ladder Company.

"Remember?" asked Charlie. "It's from the poem you were reading to me tonight: 'When out on the lawn there a rose suchak ladder'?"

"Yeah," said Scott. "From the poem." He watched, confused, as Charlie began climbing up the ladder. Then he gathered up the Santa suit and followed slowly.

Moments later, they were on the roof. Eight very large, very restless reindeer looked at them with liquid black eyes. The largest, at the head of the team, pawed the roof impatiently.

"Easy, Rudolph," said Scott.

The reindeer snorted and bucked. Its black eyes glittered.

Then Scott saw why. The tag around the animal's neck said "Comet."

"Whoops! Sorry, Comet," said Scott. Comet stopped fidgeting, and his look said that he accepted the apology.

"Dad, check out Santa's sleigh!" said Charlie as he climbed in.

"This is *not* Santa's sleigh." Scott tried to speak firmly.

"Well, what about the reindeer?"

"They . . . they're a gift from the cable company," Scott said weakly. "Merry Christmas. Now let's get off the roof."

Scott lay the Santa suit on the seat of the sleigh and stepped in to lift Charlie out. But then, as if by secret signal, all the reindeer turned their faces to the sky. With a jingle of their bells, they bounded from the roof.

"Hold on, Charlie!" was all Scott had time to yell. And then he and Charlie found themselves flying through the glittering indigo sky in Santa Claus's sleigh.

❄   ❄   ❄

Half an hour later they landed on the roof of a little house. Scott had gotten over feeling weird about what was happening. Not that he was having a good time—he just felt a little better about the situation. Easing in. And at least the reindeer seemed to know what to do. That was a relief.

So when they landed, Scott watched Comet for a cue. Sure enough, the big reindeer looked at him, and then at the bag sitting in the back of the sleigh.

"Toys!" said Charlie. "He's telling you to get the bag of toys."

"And do what?" said Scott.

"Go down the chimney," said Charlie.

"You want me to get the bag of toys and go down the chimney into a strange person's house in my pajamas?" sputtered his father.

"No," Charlie explained patiently. "You have to put the suit on first."

"Of course," said Scott sarcastically. "I'll put the suit on first. Listen, Charlie, I'll tell you what we're going to do—we're going to get out of here. This whole thing is stupid!"

"Why is it everything I want to do is stupid?" Charlie burst out.

Scott was silent a moment before he spoke. "I didn't say that," he said. Then slowly he put on the huge red suit. When he was dressed, he clambered onto the roof and grabbed the bag. It was incredibly heavy. He slipped as he pulled it out of the sleigh, and Charlie cried out in alarm.

"I'm all right, Sport," Scott said, though his voice was a little shaky. He leaned against the chimney to steady himself, wondering what to do next. How, for example, was he supposed to get down the chimney?

He didn't have much time to ponder the question. Instead, he simply started floating—first up, then down. An image of an astronaut, tumbling end over end in deep space, flashed through his mind. Frightened, he waved his arms. And then, just as his son cried, "Dad! You're flying!" he slithered down the chimney as if he were a new substance called Liquid Scott.

When he landed in the living room he felt solid again, solid enough to pull a doll, a toy rifle, and a pair of sneakers out of his bag and set them under the tree. But the minute he laid them down, he heard a deep voice from upstairs.

"Who's down there?"

Panicked, Scott tried the nearest window, which immediately set off a loud security alarm. He rushed for the door. A large dog appeared in the doorway, growling. Now what do I do?! he thought.

He got his answer when he felt himself begin to reliquify. In seconds he was floating back up the chimney. Easy as can be.

Charlie, waiting in the sleigh, looked at him wide-eyed. "Wow! Dad!" he said. "How'd you do that? What'd it feel like?"

"Like . . . *America's Most Wanted*," said Scott. "Pull me in quick! We've got to get out of here."

Scott flung his empty bag in the back of the sleigh and

flopped down next to Charlie. He snapped the reins. "Comet, let's go home!" he called. The reindeer vaulted into the sky.

But five minutes later they landed on another roof. Scott was indignant. "The bag's empty! There's nothing else!" he protested. Comet turned and growled at him. Could a reindeer growl? Comet definitely did.

"It's empty!" Scott insisted. He reached for the bag. "Look—" He picked it up. It was full.

"Dad. Do it again," said Charlie.

"But—" Scott started to protest. Then he was floating again. He panicked. "Hold it!" he yelped. "There's no chimney! Stop!"

Then he was Liquid Scott again, pouring down an exhaust vent into yet another house. When he landed he found himself standing in front of a mantel and a fireplace. Where had they come from? Scott didn't know. And how had a doll and a basketball and a jack-in-the-box gotten into his bag? Scott didn't have a clue. He noticed a glass of milk and a couple of cookies on the table, next to a plate of vegetables. Why fight it? he thought, and stashed the cookies and vegetables in his pockets.

It was only then that he noticed a little girl on the couch.

She sat up and rubbed her eyes. "Santa?" she said. "How come your clothes are so baggy?"

"Umm . . ." Scott hedged. "Santa's watching his saturated fat."

"Well, how come you don't have a beard?" the little girl persisted.

15

"I shaved!" said Scott. "Now close your eyes and go to sleep."

The little girl shut her eyes obediently. Scott sighed with relief and headed back to the chimney.

Once he was back in the sleigh again, he offered Charlie a cookie. "Hungry?" he asked.

"Starved!" Charlie said, and lunged for the cookie. Scott ate one, too, and then another. For a few minutes the only sound in the silent night was the crunch of loud, happy chewing. Then Charlie and Scott became aware of another sound—the restless pawing of eight large reindeer.

"What's the matter, boy? You hungry, too?" Scott asked Comet. The reindeer tossed its head as if to say yes. Scott pulled some vegetables out of his pocket. "Well, here you go," he said, feeding Comet a carrot.

"Let me try!" Charlie scrambled out of the sleigh. Together, he and his father walked up the row of reindeer, feeding each one a carrot or a celery stick, murmuring its name, and giving it a pat on its warm neck. The reindeer, as big as horses, became quiet as Charlie fed them. Their dark eyes seemed much softer now, and a few actually nuzzled him as he passed. It sent an unexpected thrill through Charlie. He had never had much to do with animals before, and these were so big, and so friendly! *And* they could fly!

As if thinking the same thing, Scott announced, "Well, there's work to be done, boys." He climbed back into the sleigh, waited for Charlie to settle in next to him, and took up the reins. "Now Dasher! Now Dancer! Now Prancer and Vixen!" he called. "On Comet! On Cupid! On Donner and Blitzen!" Charlie's eyes widened. His dad sounded just like Santa Claus!

The reindeer thought so, too. They vaulted into the sky with a mighty leap, and Santa's sleigh was on its way once more.

Chapter Three

It has been a long night, thought Scott. Countless deliveries, down chimneys without number. Mountains of toys coming out of a seemingly bottomless sack. Endless Christmas trees. And pounds and pounds and pounds of cookies.

Scott yawned. He was tired. So was Charlie, who was curled up next to him. It was dawn, and the sleigh had landed in a desolate white wasteland—cold, vast, and empty.

"Is this okay, Dad?" asked Charlie nervously.

"Okay? No! It's not okay!" said Scott. He flapped the reins and called out, "Hey, Comet! You made a wrong turn in Toronto! Now giddiup! Let's go home!"

Comet ignored him. For a moment the only sound Charlie and Scott heard was the keening of the wind. Then they heard something else. Footsteps. They looked around.

A tiny figure was trudging toward them through the snow. As Scott and Charlie watched, the figure came closer. It was an elf, three feet high, dressed in red and green. Without saying a word, he walked up to Comet, took hold of the harness, and urged the reindeer forward. The sleigh started to move.

"Is *this* okay, Dad?" asked Charlie.

"I think so, Sport," said Scott. "I mean, he's only an elf, right?" He called out to the tiny man. "Hello?" There was no answer. He tried again. *"Habla inglés?"* By this time the elf had led them to a snowdrift. He reached into it and pulled up a red-and-white-striped pole.

"What's that?" wondered Scott.

"I think we're at the North Pole," said Charlie. The elf found the numeric keypad on the pole and punched in a four-digit code. Nothing happened. He tried again. Nothing. Looking annoyed, the elf pulled a piece of paper out of his pocket, read the code on it, and tried again.

Suddenly Scott and Charlie heard a high, whining noise, almost like an elevator. Then they were spiraling down—sleigh, reindeer, elf, and all—in a dizzying rush of wind, mist, and snow.

When they landed and opened their eyes, they were in a huge enclosed area, rather like an airplane hangar. A crowd of elves immediately rushed over to the sleigh. They were small, serious-looking men and women wearing red and green clothing and intent expressions. Their skin, Scott noticed with surprise, had gold flecks in it. Surprisingly, too, many of them looked young. Some started to clean and polish the sleigh. Others began to groom the reindeer. No one said a word to Scott or Charlie.

Puzzled, Scott walked up to one of them. "Excuse me," he said. "Who's in charge here?"

The elf bowed at him. "You are."

"No," said Scott, "I mean, of you guys. Who's in charge?"

"You are," the elf repeated.

"That's not what I mean!" said Scott. "Who's the head elf?!"

"You are," the elf said calmly, for the third time.

Scott just stood there. Was there some mysterious elf language—Elfish?—that he just didn't understand? He was just about to try again when another elf, a slightly taller one, approached. He looked young, but had a stern face and the air of someone who's used to giving orders.

"Who's causing all the trouble around here?" he asked.

"He is," said the first elf, pointing at Scott.

"Who are you?" asked Scott.

"I'm Bernard," said the elf. "Nice to meet you, Santa."

"I'm not Santa!" Scott half-yelled.

"The other Santa is . . . gone, right?"

"Yes, but . . . ," Scott began, but the elf turned abruptly and motioned for him to follow.

Bernard headed through the hangar and down a long hallway with many doors leading off on either side.

"It wasn't my fault," Scott tried to explain as he hurried along behind the elf. "That other guy fell. It was an accident . . ."

Bernard didn't seem to be listening. "Can I get you a drink?" he asked politely.

Before Scott could answer, Charlie interrupted. "*I'm* thirsty. And hungry," he said.

The elf spun around. "Who's this?" he asked.

"My son, Charlie," said Scott.

Bernard's stern face broke into a smile. "Hiya, Sport," he said.

Charlie liked him right away. "Hey, Dad, he called me Sport," he said. "Just like you!"

"Why not?" said Bernard. "You look like a Sport. Here, I've got something for you," he said, handing Charlie a glass snowball.

There was a row of tiny plastic houses inside the ball, each with its own Christmas tree.

"Shake it up, Charlie," said the elf.

Charlie turned the ball over. Slowly it began to pulse with light, as if it were coming alive. And then it did come alive! Snow began to fall, people appeared at the windows of all the tiny houses, and Santa flew across the sky! The people waved up at his sleigh, and all the lights on the street twinkled. More snow fell, like a curtain of lace. Then it stopped, and the tiny scene went dark.

Charlie had never seen anything so beautiful. "Wow!" he whispered, handing it back to Bernard.

"Why don't you hold on to it for a while," said the elf. When Charlie hesitated, Bernard added, "Go on. I trust you to keep it safe."

"What do you say, Charlie?" said Scott, who hadn't seen the ball come alive.

"Thanks! I promise I'll take really good care of it," said Charlie.

"I know you will," said Bernard. He beckoned to one of the elves. "Larry, take Charlie with you and get him some food." Then he walked back over to Scott. "Follow me," he said. "You'll be wanting to get out of those clothes."

Scott followed Bernard through a door marked Workshop, where more elves sat at long, low benches, busily making toys. "I'll be wanting to go home!" he said, annoyed. Who did this little guy with the big attitude think he was, anyway? And why did he keep insisting Scott was Santa Claus?

"Now, look," Scott tried again. "I'm not Santa!"

"Did you or did you not read the card?" asked Bernard, stern once more.

"Well, yes I did, but—"

"Then you are the new Santa Claus," Bernard told him. "By putting on the hat and jacket you accepted the contract."

Scott was confused. "What contract?" he asked.

"The Santa Clause," said Bernard, "on the card you pulled out of Santa's wallet. Do you still have it?"

Scott found the card in his pocket and handed it to the elf.

"See? Right here in fine print," said Bernard. He started reading it to Scott. "'The Santa Clause: In putting on this suit and entering the sleigh, the wearer waives any and all rights to any previous identity, real or implied, and fully accepts the duties and responsibilities of Santa Claus in perpetuity until such time that wearer becomes unable to do so either by accident or design.' The Santa Clause," he

22

concluded. "It's all very standard."

"That's ridiculous!" Scott protested. "I'm not—"

But Bernard didn't want to hear it. "Try to understand this," he snapped. "Toys have to be delivered. I'm not going to do it, because it's not my job. It's Santa's job. But Santa fell off a roof—your roof!" He stepped closer to Scott and scowled up at him. "You read the card," he snarled. "You put on the suit. That clearly falls under the Santa Clause. So now *you* are Santa. Okay?"

Something told Scott it was useless to argue. Bernard was looking less like an elf and more like a pit bull every minute. "You leave for home tomorrow morning," he snapped. "You've got eleven months—until Thanksgiving—to get your affairs in order. Then you're due back here. I'll ship the list to your house."

"What list?" asked Scott.

The elf gave him an I-don't-believe-you look. "Come on," he said. "The *list*. As in, 'He's making a list . . .'"

"'. . . and checking it twice,'" said Charlie, who came running up to his father with his mouth full of cookies.

"That's right, Sport," said Bernard. He turned back to Scott. "You put a *P* next to the kids who were nice and a *C* next to the ones who were naughty."

"*P* and *C*?" asked Scott.

"*P* for present. *C* for coal, right?" asked Charlie.

Bernard winked at him.

Scott was puzzled. "How am I supposed to know who's—"

"You'll know," Bernard assured him.

"And what if I decide I don't want to do this?"

Bernard looked shocked. "Don't even joke about a thing like that," he said.

"Why not?" demanded Scott. "What if I don't buy into this . . . 'clause'?" What if I choose not to believe it?"

All sound in the Workshop stopped. Bernard stepped closer to Scott, his eyes glittering with anger. "Then there would be millions of disappointed children around the world," he said quietly. "Children hold the spirit of Christmas in their hearts. You wouldn't want to be responsible for killing the spirit of Christmas, *now would you?*" He jabbed Scott's stomach with a tiny finger. Scott, taken aback, was speechless.

Which was fine with Bernard, who started to march off, then stopped and added, "Judy will take you to your room. Get out of the suit. It needs to be cleaned. Then get some sleep. We've got a lot of work to do in a year."

❄   ❄   ❄

Judy was much nicer than Bernard, thought Scott. She had a friendly face. She didn't yell at him. She called him "sir," and she even brought him a cup of delicious hot cocoa as he was getting ready for bed.

And when he sat there in Santa's bedroom, dressed in Santa's very own red silk pajamas, Judy listened thoughtfully to Scott's confession.

"I stopped believing in Santa Claus a while ago," he told her, his voice troubled.

She patted his back. "Not surprising," she said. "Most grown-ups have a hard time believing in magic."

"Listen, let's be honest," Scott said. "This is a dream. You're a dream. I mean, I'm seeing this and I can't believe it."

"You're missing the point," said Judy. "Seeing isn't believing. *Believing is seeing.* Kids don't have to see this place to know that it's here. They just know."

Somehow Judy's words made Scott feel better. He also felt, suddenly, very, very tired. Judy wished him goodnight, and he settled back into bed with an enormous yawn. An instant later, he was sound asleep.

Chapter Four

"Dad! Dad!" Scott woke abruptly to the sound of Charlie's voice calling from the hallway. "You should see all the toys," cried his son, bursting into the bedroom. "Come on, get up. Get up!"

There was no time to think about his unusual red silk pajamas or his strange dream of elves and sleighs and reindeer because Charlie was pulling him downstairs into the living room, where a mountain of brightly wrapped presents lay under the tree. Scott had no idea where they'd come from; Charlie didn't care. He just started to open them as fast as he could.

Then the doorbell rang, and Charlie ran to answer it. "Mom!" he cried, greeting Laura happily.

"Did you have a good time?" she asked, surprised at his cheerful expression. Usually he couldn't even manage a smile when she picked him up at Scott's. Today he was beaming.

"A great time!" he told her. "Dad and me and the reindeer flew up to the North Pole. Dad was Santa, and Larry showed me the Workshop. It was neat, Mom, really! You should have been there."

Laura glared at Scott, who stood there bleary-eyed in his red pajamas. She sent Charlie out to the car, where Neal was waiting, and then turned to her ex-husband.

"Scott!" she hissed. "What kind of stories have you been filling Charlie's head with? The North Pole! Santa! Really!"

Scott scratched his head. "I'm not filling his head with anything," he said. "I thought it was a dream. . . ."

Then it hit him. How could it have been a dream if Charlie knew about the Workshop and the elves? He ran out to the car.

"Sport!" he said to Charlie, who was in the backseat. "Who showed you the Workshop?"

"Larry," said Charlie matter-of-factly.

"What was the other one's name?" asked Scott.

"Bernard."

"And who gave me the pajamas?"

"Judy," said his son. "Why?"

"What's this all about?" asked Neal with a frown.

"Dad took me to the North Pole," Charlie told him. "He's the new Santa, because the regular Santa fell off our roof."

Scott stood there, dumbfounded. "But it was a dream," he said.

Laura and Neal scowled at him and then drove away. "It couldn't have happened," he yelled after them. But as he watched them disappear down the street, he wrestled with a thought so incredible that it made his scalp tingle. Maybe his dream wasn't really a dream. Maybe the Santa Clause was real!

❄   ❄   ❄

A few weeks later, Scott sat in the conference room of the B and R Toy Company staring at the plate of cookies across the table. Ever since Christmas, Scott had found himself on a new diet—the Milk and Cookies Diet—and his craving for cookies seemed to be getting stronger with every passing day.

The sight of an entire plate of chocolate chip cookies just out of his reach was very frustrating. He'd been signaling for them over and over again! But no one at the table noticed. All eyes were on the boss, Mr. Whittle, as he made a speech about a new B and R toy.

"It is with much pleasure and pride that I announce our next best-seller," he boomed. "B and R's Total Tank. This is our high-end male action toy for next Christmas, which we hope to retail at $159.00 . . ."

As Mr. Whittle droned on, Scott forgot about the cookies, the meeting, and the high-end action toys. He began to doodle a glass snowball, just like the one Bernard had given Charlie at the North Pole. As he drew, he could almost swear he heard bells jingling—sleigh bells. . . .

Then all of a sudden he heard his name being called. He looked up.

The entire room was staring at him. Mr. Whittle was staring especially hard. Scott didn't like that look. It meant something was wrong.

"Yes, Mr. Whittle?" he asked innocently, dropping his pencil.

"The Total Tank focus group, Scott?" said Mr. Whittle.

"Yes, sir," said Scott. "It was last week."

"I *know*! Do you have the report?" Mr. Whittle's face was turning all blotchy and red.

"Yes, I do." Scott shuffled through his papers. "I, uh . . . I must have left it in my office," he said.

"Well, if it wouldn't be too much trouble," said Mr. Whittle, "would you find it and bring it to us, since *we are all waiting*?"

Scott jumped to his feet. "Sorry. Be right back with it." As he left the room, he turned back for a moment. "Anyone else hear those bells?" he asked.

Dead silence.

"The report," said Scott. "Right. I'll be back in a second."

❊   ❊   ❊

Ever since their night in the sleigh, Charlie felt different about his dad. He used to pity him for messing up so much. He was angry with him a lot, too, for the same reason. But after seeing him deliver all those presents, Charlie began to feel proud of his dad. After all, he had an incredibly important job to do! Maybe the most important job of anyone!

So when Scott walked into his classroom on Career Day, Charlie was really surprised and pleased. There were other parents there, too, of course, including Charlie's mom and Neal. But their jobs weren't half as interesting as Scott's. Not that there was anything wrong with being a psychiatrist like Neal. Charlie even used to think it was kind of cool. And his mom's job, travel agent, was fine, too. But now they seemed a little ordinary to Charlie.

Nothing like being Santa.

He couldn't wait to introduce his father. So as soon as Scott sat down, Charlie walked up to the front of the classroom.

"This is my dad, Scott Calvin," he said.

"Hello, Mr. Calvin," droned the class.

"And what does your dad do?" asked the teacher, Ms. Daniels.

"My dad is Santa Claus," Charlie said proudly.

Everyone started laughing. Scott jumped up. He had seen the looks of outrage on Neal's and Laura's faces. He had to do something fast.

"I think what Charlie means," he said to everyone, "is that I'm *like* Santa."

"That's *not* what I mean, dad," said Charlie. He turned to the class. "Look, on Christmas Eve my dad pushed Santa off the roof. Santa disappeared and my dad took his place. Then the reindeer flew us to the North Pole, where the head elf, Bernard, gave me this." He pulled the glass ball from his backpack.

Scott interrupted. "Listen," he said to the class, "I work for a toy company. And in a way I deliver toys all over the country, like Santa . . ."

"Do you make the toys?" asked a girl from the back of the room.

"No, stupid," sneered Bobby Turrell, a kid who had two jobs: class know-it-all and class bully. "The *elves* do."

The class laughed again. "The toys are made some-where else," Scott explained. "At a factory overseas."

Bobby ignored his answer. "So, let me get this straight," he jeered. "If I want to be Santa when I grow up, all I have to do is push you off a roof?"

The class burst into laughter again.

But Scott noticed Laura and Neal weren't laughing.

❄   ❄   ❄

The next morning Scott sat in the principal's office with Laura and Neal. He tried to explain.

"First of all," he said, "I didn't push Santa. He fell."

Laura was outraged. "Why are you doing this, Scott?" she asked. "Why's Charlie making up all these stories? Why's he saying this is the best Christmas he's ever had?"

"He said that?" Scott was surprised—and touched.

"After everything you've told him? Of course he did!"

"This is far more serious than a boy believing or not believing in Santa Claus," Principal Compton inter-rupted.

"Charlie thinks it really happened," Laura added.

"Look," said Scott in his most reasonable tone of voice. "It *was* Christmas, right? So it makes sense that I had some holiday fantasy pop into my head. I must have told Charlie. He must have liked it. End of story."

"And did you go to the North Pole?" asked Neal accus-ingly.

"This is ridiculous," said Scott.

"Ridiculous or not," said the principal, "for Charlie this

isn't some dream. It's real. You need to sit down with Charlie, Mr. Calvin. Explain to him that you're not Santa Claus and *get through to him*. No matter what it takes."

Scott got the message. He was going to have a little talk with Charlie. Soon.

"Hey, you!" Scott shouts at the man who's fallen from the roof and is lying in the snow.

Scott and Charlie can't believe their eyes! A large sleigh harnessed with eight reindeer is standing next to their chimney.

Eight reindeer and a sleigh on the roof? This is going to be the best Christmas Eve ever!

It is Christmas Eve, and little does Scott know that once he dons the huge red Santa suit, there's no turning back!

"Whoa!" Without even trying, Scott floats up into the sky and slithers down the chimney to deliver his first bagful of toys.

On solid ground again, Scott is glad not to feel like *Liquid Scott* anymore!

"Now, Dasher! Now, Dancer! Now, Prancer and Vixen! On, Comet! On, Cupid! On, Donner and Blitzen!"

Bernard gives Charlie a magic glass snowball.

Bernard explains the Santa Clause to Scott.

Scott thinks this whole night is just a dream, but is he willing to take the chance of disappointing millions of children around the world?

Becoming rounder and rounder and more Santa-like every day, Scott wonders why the B and R Toy Company doesn't make good toys like the glass ball anymore.

Charlie can do anything he sets his mind to.... Believing is seeing!

In Santa's bedroom at the North Pole, rows and rows of portraits of previous Santas, trapped by the Santa Clause, adorn the walls.

Laura's, Charlie's, and Neal's Christmas dreams all come true!

Charlie can be with his dad—the one-and-only Santa Claus—anytime he misses him. All he has to do is shake the magic glass snowball!

Chapter Five

The following Saturday, Scott and Charlie were together again, and Scott meant to talk to his son. But not right away—he didn't want to spoil their day. Scott had brought home a new Total Tank toy so that he and Charlie could assemble it together. And now, here they were, in the living room, trying to do just that. But they weren't getting very far.

The Total Tank had about nine million little parts, and they were scattered all over the floor. The instruction book was as thick as a phone book and a lot more confusing.

"I hate kits," announced Charlie. "They have millions of parts that never work. They break ten seconds after you build them. And you always end up spending more money to get new parts."

"But the important thing is that we're doing this together," said Scott, trying to sound enthusiastic. Charlie's response was a yawn and a grunt.

After an hour of trying to follow the instructions, even Scott had to admit defeat. There were nine wing nuts instead of ten. He couldn't tell the difference between the driveshaft and the wheelbase. And Charlie, totally bored, was watching television.

"Hey, Sport, I feel like going out," Scott said finally. "What do you say we go to the zoo?"

Fifteen minutes later they were walking past the reindeer pen, heading for the polar bears.

"These are just like the bears at the North Pole," said Charlie, staring wistfully at the big shaggy creatures.

Here's my chance! thought Scott. "Charlie," he began, "I've already told you we never went to the North Pole. Remember? It was all just a dream."

"Nah," said Charlie. "It happened."

Scott kept trying. "I can't explain it," he said. "But I know what happened wasn't real."

"It *was* real," said Charlie.

"How do you know?" demanded Scott. "There's no proof. So why don't we just say it was a great dream and forget it?"

"Proof?" Charlie smiled. "What about this?" He held out the glass ball Bernard had given him, the one that lit up and had snow falling inside it. It wasn't lit up now, though.

Scott turned the ball over in his hands. "This is just a cheap toy," he said. "We used to make these at B and R. Years ago."

Charlie knew the ball was magic. If his dad couldn't see it now, he would before too long. Just the way he'd realize he was Santa. He had to.

"I know who you are, Dad," he said. "You'll figure it

out soon enough. There are a lot of kids who believe in you. You can't let them down."

Scott's heart sank. He wasn't getting anywhere. "Charlie, you're wrong," he protested. To his surprise, his son was smiling again.

"What's so funny?" he asked.

"Nothing," said Charlie. There was no way he'd tell his father that eight reindeer, zoo reindeer, were lined up in pairs behind them. Had they jumped over the fence of their pen? Or flown over? Who knew? But one thing was dead certain to Charlie. The reindeer were following his dad. Correction, he thought. The reindeer are following Santa. His grin got even wider.

So much for our little talk, thought Scott.

❄   ❄   ❄

A few weeks later Scott found himself having another little talk. This one wasn't with Charlie. It was with Mr. Whittle, his boss. In its way, it was just as disturbing.

It started off with Mr. Whittle complaining. He'd been doing a lot of that lately. This time he was upset because Scott was eating milk and cookies instead of sending out the Christmas orders of Total Tanks.

"I just got off the phone with Dale Jenkins," Mr. Whittle said, "and he told me something I couldn't believe. He told me you haven't shipped him the Total Tank yet."

Scott sat at his desk and munched on a cookie. "Oh, yes," he said. "I was going to talk to you about that."

"Talk?" exclaimed Mr. Whittle. "What is there to talk about? He's a toy buyer. We send him a toy and he buys!"

Scott picked up the glass ball that sat on his desk. "Well, you know, Mr. Whittle," he said, "I was looking at the Tank and I was wondering . . . is it really the kind of toy an eight year old would like?"

Mr. Whittle opened his mouth to answer. Then he noticed the ball in Scott's hands. "What's that?" he asked.

"It's my son's," said Scott. "We used to make them here. Why did we stop?"

Mr. Whittle stared at Scott. His pale blue eyes widened, and his round, puffy face turned red. He looked like a fifty-year-old baby getting ready to scream.

"Why?" he answered loudly. "I'll tell you why! Because it doesn't shoot, explode, kill, or talk. It doesn't change into anything, fly, drive, glow in the dark, ooze, or stick to the walls, that's why! It just sits there! *Now send that sample*!"

And he stormed out.

❋   ❋   ❋

A few days later, Neal decided it was his turn to try to have a talk with Charlie. He sat next to his stepson on the living room couch, being as reasonable as he could. But Charlie just didn't seem to want to listen to what he was saying. No matter how logical it was.

Neal picked up a globe. "Let's try again." Pointing to the top, he said, "Here's the North Pole. And here's the rest of the world." He pointed again. "Now, how can one man visit all the children of the world in one night? It isn't logical. It's impossible."

"Not everyone celebrates Christmas," said Charlie.

"And that upsets you?" asked Neal. Maybe Charlie was listening to him after all.

"No," said Charlie. "Not everyone celebrates Christmas. So Santa doesn't have to visit *everyone*."

Neal sighed. "Well, what about fireplaces?" he asked. "A lot of people don't have them. How does Santa visit those people?"

"He turns into Jell-O and a fireplace just kind of appears," said Charlie without hesitation.

"Okay," said Neal. "What about the reindeer? Have you ever seen reindeer fly?" he asked a little desperately.

"Yes."

"Well, I haven't," said Neal.

"Have you ever seen a million dollars?" asked Charlie.

"No."

"Just because you haven't seen it doesn't mean it doesn't exist," said Charlie with irrefutable logic.

This is really out of control, thought Neal. At that moment Scott and Laura appeared in the doorway. Scott had stopped by to pick up Charlie for the afternoon.

"Hi, Sport," he said to his son. "Feel like taking a walk with your old man?"

Charlie was glad to see him. "Do I ever," he said. "I'll get my jacket."

Charlie dashed out of the room. Scott turned to follow, but Laura stopped him.

"Scott, how can you tell these ridiculous stories to Charlie?" she asked. "You *have* to tell him the truth."

"The truth . . . ?" But I don't know what the truth is, thought Scott. Maybe I *am* Santa Claus!

"Yes, be honest with him, Scott," said Neal. He and Laura exchanged worried glances. "Because I'm really concerned."

"About what?" asked Scott, bristling.

"About whether it's good for Charlie to spend time with you," said Neal.

It was a threat, and Scott knew it.

Chapter Six

Later that afternoon Scott and Charlie sat across the street from the house they had lived in before Scott and Laura's divorce.

"Funny," said Charlie. "It looks smaller to me now."

"Maybe you're just bigger," said Scott.

"Yeah," agreed Charlie. "Hey!" he added. "By next year, I'll be big enough to fly the sleigh all by myself!"

Scott winced. "No!" he protested.

"Okay, okay," said Charlie. "The year after."

"No. That's not what I meant." Scott took Charlie by the shoulders. "Sport," he said, "we've got to get something straight about this Santa business. There is no—" He couldn't finish.

"No what?"

The words *There is no Santa Claus* refused to come out of Scott's mouth. Instead, he said, "There is no reason why you should tell people about the North Pole."

"Why not?"

Scott didn't want to tell Charlie to lie. "Well, because sometimes there are things . . . big things . . . that are better left unsaid."

"You mean like a secret?" asked Charlie.

"YES!" exclaimed Scott. "That's it! A secret. Right!" He looked his son in the eye. "Let's keep it a secret."

"Why?" asked Charlie.

"Well, you know, Mom and Neal feel . . . And not just Mom and Neal . . . There's the school—not that it's important what they think, but you know . . ." Scott's voice trailed off for a moment. "I need you to do this for me, Sport," he said finally. "Will you? Please?"

Charlie was flattered. His father had never asked him for anything before. This would be hard, but he'd do it. "Sure, Dad," he said.

Scott beamed with relief. Finally, he thought, life would be normal again.

But Scott was wrong.

Things were far from normal, as he found out the next morning.

His weight, for instance, had suddenly jumped to 190 pounds. His normal weight was 160. His hair was turning gray, and he had grown a beard—overnight! Scott didn't understand it, and he didn't like it.

He had other problems, too. Big ones. None of his clothes fit, and he was late for an important meeting. He had to race to the office dressed in an old sweat suit that was much too small for him. And once he was actually at the meeting, things got even worse.

Everyone there looked shocked when he came into the conference room, so he told them he was dressed in sweats because his dry cleaners had burned to the ground—with all his clothes in it.

Then Mr. Whittle asked him how he'd put on so much

weight, and he had to make up another story, this time about having an allergic reaction to a bee sting.

He could tell no one believed him, either. It was terrible.

It was terrible, too, when they all ordered lunch. Because even though he meant to order sensible, healthy food like everyone else—Caesar salad, no dressing— when the waiter came to him, Scott heard himself asking for cookies, a hot fudge sundae with extra fudge, and an order of cheesecake on the side. Everyone stared at him, horrified.

It got worse.

The purpose of the meeting was to look at the plans for the new Total Tank TV commercial. Like all toy commercials, this one cost a lot of money, and everyone took it very seriously—the people from B and R, and the man from the advertising agency.

It began with a shot of Santa Claus at the North Pole, and as soon as Scott saw it he laughed.

Silence fell over the conference room.

"Is there a problem?" asked the man from the ad agency.

"No, nothing," said Scott. "Nothing." Unfortunately, he couldn't stop there. "It's a little thing," he added. "The elves."

"What about them?"

"They look funny," said Scott.

"They're supposed to. They're elves," said the advertising man curtly.

"I know that," said Scott. "But they should look

41

younger. And their skin should have gold flecks in it."

"Pardon me?" said the advertising man.

"You know, gold flecks in their skin," Scott said again, as if this were common knowledge about elves.

The advertising man chose not to answer Scott. Instead he turned to the second shot in the commercial, a picture of Santa in the Total Tank. "This year," he said proudly, "Santa's not going in his sleigh. He's going in a Total Tank! We think it's a great concept."

"Now wait a minute," said Scott. All heads swiveled his way. "Not that *I* know anything about Santa Claus," he continued, "but there is *absolutely no way* Santa would give up his sleigh."

"He would if he was trying to sell the Total Tank," said the advertising man, shooting Mr. Whittle an I-don't-believe-this-joker look.

Scott ignored him. "Look, he needs his reindeer, right? Who do you think knows the way to all those houses but the reindeer? Santa can't do all those things himself. I mean, after all, he's only human—I guess."

"Calvin!" interrupted Mr. Whittle.

"I'm not finished!" Scott was standing now, addressing everyone in the room. "While we're discussing the Total Tank," he said, "have any of you tried putting it together?" He looked around the room. No one said a word. "Well, let me tell you: nuclear fusion is simpler. Even if you do manage to assemble the thing, it doesn't work. It breaks ten seconds after you build it. So you have to spend even more money on new parts. Ridiculous."

"Calvin!" Mr. Whittle got to his feet a little unsteadily

and glared at Scott. "I'd like to see you outside—"

"What we should try to come up with," Scott went on, "is a simple, basic, affordable toy. Something that nurtures creativity—"

"NOW!" exploded Mr. Whittle. Grabbing Scott by the collar of his sweat suit, he dragged him into the hallway. "I don't know what's gotten into you, Calvin," he fumed. "You're fat. That beard is a disgrace. And you're acting crazy. I mean, *gold flecks*?!"

"You're right," said Scott apologetically. "I don't know what got into me."

"Well, do something about it," said Mr. Whittle. "Go see a doctor or something. Get some help. Soon!"

❅ ❅ ❅

Dr. Meyers had been treating Scott and the Calvin family for years. He was a plump, easygoing man who gave all his patients chocolate lollipops. Scott liked him.

And he liked hearing what Dr. Meyers had to say. "Scott, you're healthy as a horse. What's the problem?"

Scott smiled, relieved. "No problem, really," he said. "Actually, I'm feeling great." He waited for his chocolate lollipop.

But Dr. Meyers wasn't quite finished with him. "You've put on some weight since I saw you last year," he said. "What's your diet like?"

"Mostly cookies and milk," confessed Scott. He liked to think of it as a vegetarian diet, only better.

"Well, there it is," said the doctor. "Try to cut back on the sweets, okay?" He smiled at Scott. "Anything else?"

"There is one thing," said Scott. "How fast should facial hair grow?" He rubbed his full beard.

"It varies from person to person," said the doctor. "Why?"

"Well . . . I shaved this morning."

Dr. Meyers frowned and checked Scott's thyroid gland. "Hmmm . . . normal," he murmured. "Try another kind of razor, I guess."

"Also," said Scott, "as you can see, my hair's turned gray."

The doctor smiled. "You can dye it," he said. "Now let's take a listen to the old ticker, okay?"

Dr. Meyers put the stethoscope to Scott's chest. Scott's heart sounded normal—at first. But after a moment the rhythm changed. Dr. Meyer's eyes widened as he listened. There was no mistaking it. Scott's heart was pumping out the tune to "Jingle Bells."

Chapter Seven

Several weeks later, on a Saturday in early spring, Scott decided to stroll over to the park. Now that he'd seen Dr. Meyers, he'd stopped worrying. It was a beautiful day, and he was on his way to watch Charlie play soccer.

When Charlie saw Scott, he ran right over to him. "Hey, Dad, what're you doing here?" he asked, sounding surprised. He looked pleased, too. His father had never bothered to come to the soccer field before.

"I dunno," said Scott. "I thought I'd see what this soccer stuff is all about. Lots of people play it, right? Including you. So it must have something. And I kind of like the idea of seeing you bounce a ball off your head, Sport." He grinned.

Charlie grinned back. "This is great, Dad," he said. "You can come whenever you want."

Just then a pink rubber ball bounced by Scott's feet. A dark-haired girl came running after it. Scott picked up the ball, tossed it to the girl, and called, "There you go, Ruth."

"Thanks," she said, a little startled.

Charlie stared at his father. "How did you know her name?" he asked.

"Gee, I don't know," said Scott. He scratched his head, just as puzzled as Charlie. "Look," he said, "I'll just go sit over there on that bench. Where that other little girl is sitting."

"Fine." Charlie ran back to his game, and Scott settled down to watch. But before two minutes had passed, he realized that the little girl on the bench was staring at him. Hard. She had curly red hair and a band of freckles across her nose.

"What is it?" he asked her.

She climbed onto his lap. "I want some ballet shoes," she whispered into his ear.

And she was just the first. Before Scott knew how or why, there was a line of kids waiting beside his bench. One by one they climbed onto his lap and told him what they wanted for Christmas. A few were shy, a few were funny, and one or two seemed to want half the toys made in the United States. But the surprising thing was that Scott knew everyone's name, and he liked them all. Not a single lump of coal in the bunch, he thought, smiling.

Then he heard a shriek. It was Laura.

She stood over him, hair flying. "You have really gone too far, Scott," she yelled. Neal, rushing up behind her, nodded vigorously in agreement.

Scott put little Hector down. "I'm not finished yet," protested the boy.

"Fax me a list," Scott told him, taking Laura and Neal

aside. He tried to explain what was going on. It wasn't easy, since he wasn't too sure himself.

"This isn't what you think," he said. "The kids just came up to me."

"Look at you!" gasped Laura. "Your hair! Your weight!"

Neal nodded. "I think you're taking this Santa thing to an unhealthy level," he said.

"This is really starting to scare me," added Laura.

"Scare you?" asked Scott. "So I've put on a few pounds and my hair's gray—big deal! Dr. Meyers says I'm fine—"

"I never thought you'd stoop to changing your physical appearance to make Charlie like you," Laura interrupted. "You have no idea of how dangerous this is to a little boy."

Once again Neal nodded in agreement. Scott could practically see him making a spiral with his index finger—the "he's cuckoo" sign. Not that Neal had to. His opinion of Scott was written all over his face.

Scott didn't like where this was leading. His stomach did an Olympic-force flip. "Dangerous?" he said. "Whoa, now, wait a minute—"

Charlie ran over, and the three adults fell silent. "What's wrong?" he asked.

"We're going home," said Laura, taking hold of his arm.

Charlie pulled away, looking pleadingly at his dad. "But the game just started."

Laura took hold of him again. "We're going home," she repeated firmly. Halfway to the car she turned and called, "You'd better get your act together, Scott . . ."

". . . or else," finished Neal.

Scott just stood there. He was so worried he couldn't even snap back at Neal.

He was still standing there when a little boy walked up. "Hey, Santa!" the boy said. "What's your fax number?"

Chapter Eight

A few months later, Scott stood in the bathroom getting ready to shave. As he'd explained to Dr. Meyers, his normal razor wasn't working anymore—he'd shave in the morning and his beard would be full again by afternoon. So yesterday Scott bought an expensive new European model—sleek and black with three sets of shiny silver blades. "It's the best we have," the salesman had said. Scott hoped so. It cost as much as a television set.

He lathered his face and began to shave. The new razor disposed of his entire beard in just under two minutes. This is more like it! thought Scott, admiring his face in the mirror.

The doorbell rang.

Scott hurried downstairs. The mail carrier was waiting outside. "Delivery for S.C.," he said. "You S.C.?"

"Scott Calvin, that's me. Who's it from?"

"No return address," said the mail carrier. "I'll get your packages. There's quite a few."

"Just leave them in the hallway," said Scott. He hurried upstairs, eager to see himself clean shaven again.

He looked in the mirror.

"NO!" It was a half-scream, half-gasp of astonishment. But it didn't change what Scott saw in the mirror—a roly-poly man with rosy cheeks, a full white beard, and a head of snowy white hair. The man in the mirror was—

The front door slammed, reminding Scott about the mail carrier and the packages. He ran downstairs to find his hallway filled to the ceiling with cardboard boxes. A note was taped to one of them. "Here's the list," it said. "Check it. Twice! Yours, B."

Scott opened the first box. It was filled with a thick sheaf of paper covered with names in alphabetical order—children's names.

Scott looked up and saw his reflection in the hallway mirror—a roly-poly man with rosy cheeks, a full white beard, and a head of snowy white hair, holding a list of names. The man in the mirror was—

"NO!" This time it came out as a whimper. There's been a mistake, thought Scott. A postal error! The mail carrier must have come to the wrong address.

He ran outside, but the mail truck was at the end of the street and moving fast. "Hey, you! Come back here!" yelled Scott. But the truck kept right on going.

Scott stood there in his red silk bathrobe. He was covered with goose bumps. They weren't from the wind, cooler now that summer was ending. They were from sheer, downright perplexity. Who *was* he? He just didn't know anymore.

❆   ❆   ❆

Charlie wasn't confused about who his father was. He was Santa, no question. Charlie also understood he had to keep that a secret. So when his mom offered to take him camping that weekend, Charlie answered carefully.

"I can't," he said. "I'm going to be with Dad."

Laura was surprised. "You can skip this weekend," she said. "He probably wouldn't mind. Unless you had something special planned."

"We're cleaning out his garage," said Charlie. He didn't tell her why. She wouldn't understand about all the cardboard boxes filled with the gigantic list—Santa's list—sitting in his dad's hallway. The boxes had to be put away in the garage before anyone saw them. They were part of the secret, too.

"Wait a minute!" said Laura. "Are you telling me you'd rather clean out your father's garage than go camping?"

"Yup."

Laura looked at her son. "Charlie, you used to hate going to your dad's house. What's changed?"

"Dad," said Charlie. "He's different now."

"I know!" said Laura, rolling her eyes.

"Good," said Charlie. "Then you understand." And that was all he would say, no matter what his mom asked him.

He had to keep the secret.

❄   ❄   ❄

It was much harder at school.

Charlie found that out one day in October.

He was at his desk after recess, looking for the glass ball

Bernard had given him. He'd put it in his pack that morning. But now it wasn't there.

He searched the pack again, fighting a sick feeling in his stomach. The glass ball meant a lot to him. He couldn't have lost it!

"Looking for this?" Bobby Turrell tapped him on the shoulder with the glass ball, then snatched it away when Charlie grabbed for it.

"Hey!" said Charlie. "Give that to me!"

Bobby was good at being the class bully. He taunted Charlie with the ball, waving it just out of his reach and smirking. "What's the big deal with this thing anyway?" he sneered. "It's just a stupid paperweight."

"I promised I'd take care of it," said Charlie.

"Promised who? Ber*nard*?" mocked Bobby.

One part of Charlie wondered why Bobby liked making him miserable. Another part just wanted to kick his butt. "Give me the ball, okay?" He tried not to sound like he was pleading.

Bobby laughed. "No wa-ay," he sang. "I'm gonna keep it. And you better not say anything, elf boy."

By now the other kids were coming in from recess. Then Ms. Daniels came in and told everyone to sit down.

Charlie sat. He knew he couldn't say anything to his teacher. He had to keep the secret.

It wasn't easy being the son of Santa.

✵　　✵　　✵

Charlie might have cheered up, though, if he'd been with Scott later that week.

Scott was having a good time. His day at B and R started with a pleasant surprise. A group of kids had been called in to test the Total Tank, and they hated it. So Mr. Whittle was actually apologizing to Scott. This was a first. It was fun.

"You were right," Mr. Whittle told him, looking embarrassed. "And I'm sorry I lost my temper with you. The kids do hate the Tank, Scott. I . . . uh . . . I'm hoping that with some design changes, maybe some of the things you suggested, we could reissue it next year. What do you think?"

Scott's eyes twinkled. "Actually, Mr. Whittle, I don't know if I'll be here next year," he said. "I might have to leave B and R."

"Leave! You mean you have a better offer somewhere else?" Mr. Whittle sounded slightly alarmed. Scott had been right about the Total Tank. He could be right about other things. B and R needed him.

"Not exactly," said Scott. "It just looks as if . . . as if I might have to distribute some toys soon."

"Sounds like another job to me," said Mr. Whittle. "Local outfit?"

"Up north."

"What are they offering you, Calvin? I'll—I'll match it!" Now that Scott was actually quitting, Mr. Whittle didn't want him to go. "What's the position?"

Scott's eyes twinkled a little more brightly. "Santa Claus," he said.

Mr. Whittle swallowed. He opened his mouth but no words came out, so he rolled his desk chair as far away from Scott as it would go. He had never had to deal with an employee who had lost his mind before. It was frightening.

"You're fired," he finally managed to say.

❄   ❄   ❄

Once Scott actually admitted that he might be Santa, he found himself in a much better frame of mind. He stopped worrying about his weight, and his beard, and his hair. He stopped shaving. He began checking the Christmas list, which was now safely in his garage. And on this particular morning he was really looking forward to seeing Charlie. They had made a date to choose a Halloween pumpkin to carve together—just the two of them.

But by the time they got to the pumpkin field, Scott knew something was wrong. Charlie was hardly talking. He wouldn't say anything about school. And his eyes were sad.

Scott sat down on a pumpkin in the middle of the field and took Charlie's hand. "You okay?" he asked.

"Yeah," Charlie mumbled, eyes down. He was a terrible liar.

"What is it, Charlie? Tell me," said Scott.

For a minute Charlie didn't say anything. Then he sat down on a pumpkin next to his father. "There's this kid," he began, "in school. He took something of mine." He looked at Scott. "He took that glass ball Bernard gave me."

Charlie waited for his father to say, "There's no glass ball. There's no Bernard. I'm not Santa. It was all a dream." His stomach tightened up. He couldn't stand to hear those words.

He didn't. All Scott said was, "Go on."

"I told him to give it back. He wouldn't."

"Did you tell your teacher?"

Charlie shook his head no.

"Why not?"

"Our secret, Dad," said Charlie. "You made me promise never to talk about North Pole stuff. Ever. And he'll kill me if I rat on him. He's big. Real big."

"Bigger than me?" asked Scott.

"Dad," said Charlie, "*no one's* bigger than you."

❄   ❄   ❄

Later, as they carved a wonderful frightening face into their jack-o'-lantern, Scott continued their conversation. "Charlie, why is that glass ball so important to you?"

Charlie hoped his dad would understand. "Because . . . because of the magic," he said.

"The magic," repeated Scott. He smiled. "You believe in that magic, don't you?"

"More than anything," said Charlie.

"Charlie," said Scott, "if you believe in it so much, then you have to do something. Even if it means telling the secret."

"But I can't tell!" said Charlie. "You said—"

"I was wrong," Scott said firmly. "I shouldn't have

made you keep that secret. I was trying to make things easier for me. But all I did was make them harder for you."

"That's okay," Charlie said quickly.

"No. I don't ever want you to be afraid to stand up for something you believe in, Sport. That's much more important than keeping secrets. But if this kid is *really* that big . . . maybe I—"

"Dad! Don't you think I can do it myself?"

"Sport," said Scott, "I believe you can do just about anything you set your mind to. Anything."

Now it was Charlie's turn to smile. "You *are* Santa, aren't you, Dad?"

Scott put his arm around his son. "When it comes right down to it," he said, "it doesn't matter whether I am or not. But the way we're talking? That matters. *That's* important."

And Charlie knew he meant it.

Chapter Nine

Not long after that, on a crisp November afternoon, Scott strolled through the neighborhood, enjoying the sunshine and thinking about his list. He'd gotten more than halfway through it, and he was pleased at how many kids had been good this year. He wondered if the list were longer than usual and decided to ask Bernard when he got back to the North Pole.

Scott turned a corner and saw a burly man who was trying to open up the back of his pickup truck while holding a large box. Scott stopped to help him, taking the box so the man could use both hands on the truck.

As Scott took the box, he realized it was a Total Tank. At the same time, he saw a boy about Charlie's age sitting in the truck. It was Bobby Turrell. Bobby the Bully.

An impish smile passed over Scott's face. "Total Tank, huh?" he said to Bobby. "Good luck."

Bobby scowled at Scott. Then he recognized him. "Hey!" he said. "You're Charlie's dad."

"Hi, Bobby," said Scott casually. Then he snapped his fingers as if he'd just remembered something. "Whoa!

Bobby Turrell!" he exclaimed. "You've been one *very* naughty boy this year, haven't you?"

Bobby looked surprised, then sullen. "I didn't do nothing," he muttered.

Mr. Turrell came over. "What're you talking about?" he asked, taking the box back from Scott.

"I don't know," said Scott. "It's the weirdest thing. It just came to me out of the blue." And he walked off.

"What was that all about?" demanded Mr. Turrell.

Bobby fumed. He'd get Charlie for this, the little rat fink!

❄   ❄   ❄

Bobby found Charlie the next day, in the computer room. Charlie was working on a computer drawing of a sleigh and eight reindeer when Bobby yanked him out of his seat and into the hallway.

"What's wrong?" asked Charlie. Bobby looked even more scary than usual.

"You told! You told your dad it was me." Bobby loomed over Charlie clenching and unclenching his fists.

"Did not," said Charlie, standing his ground.

"He practically attacked me on the street, gave me all this stuff about being naughty. How'd he know if you didn't tell?"

"He must have been reading the list," said Charlie.

"What list?"

"The 'who's been naughty and nice' list," Charlie said patiently.

Bobby looked confused. "Your dad has a list?"

"Of course he does," said Charlie. "He's Santa Claus!"

That did it. Bobby threw Charlie down on the floor and crouched over him. "THERE IS NO SANTA CLAUS! Say it!"

"No," said Charlie, trying to get up.

"Say it!" Bobby pushed him down again, harder this time.

"NO!" Charlie tried to struggle up, and Bobby punched him. Charlie backed off on his knees and slowly made it to his feet, breathing hard. His nose was bleeding.

This time Bobby hit Charlie hard in the chest with both hands, knocking him backward. "There is no Santa!" he insisted. "THERE IS NO SANTA!"

Charlie was panting too hard to speak, but they both knew he wasn't going to quit. "Yes, there is," he finally managed to gasp.

Suddenly a voice came from the top of the stairs. "Yes, there is," it said.

"Yes, there is," said another voice from down the hall.

Bobby and Charlie looked up—and saw that a group of kids had come out of the computer room. "Yes, there is," said LaWanda. She was the biggest girl in their class, and her voice rang like a bell in the hallway. A murmur of agreement came from the others, who joined her to stand behind Charlie.

Bobby's eyes darted to the Exit door at the end of the hall. *He's afraid!* thought Charlie. All of a sudden he felt great.

"Give me my ball," he said to Bobby.

Bobby stared at him. "You want your ball?" he sneered.

"Your precious glass ball? Sure! I'll give it to you." He went to his locker and pulled it out. "In a million pieces, dork!" And he pitched the ball toward the Exit as hard as he could.

Charlie watched numbly as the ball sailed through the air. How could he ever have expected to win against Bobby Turrell? How? He closed his eyes as if he could keep from hearing the glass ball shatter. Suddenly, in his mind, he saw his dad's face, smiling at him. "I believe you can do whatever you set your mind to, Sport," he heard his dad say, and Charlie's heart lifted.

After that it was simple. Keeping his eyes closed, Charlie pictured the glass ball as he'd first seen it, pulsing with magical light. Come back! he thought. Come back! Please!

The hallway was so quiet you could hear the wall clock ticking. Charlie opened his eyes and looked up. The glass ball hovered near the ceiling, glowing. Then it floated down into his hand like some giant jewel.

"Whoa . . ." A soft, awestruck murmur came from all the kids in the hallway.

Charlie's hands closed around the ball. It flickered once, as if greeting him, and went dark.

He smiled at Bobby. "Thanks," he said, getting up and leading the other kids back into the computer room. Life was good sometimes.

❄   ❄   ❄

Charlie was still in an excellent mood when he got home

from school, but he had a hard time explaining why to his mom. For some reason the blood on his shirt really upset her. And when he told her about the fight and how great it was, she didn't understand at all. She kept asking him boring questions, like how he had gotten into a fight in the first place.

"Well," he said, "Bobby Turrell said I told Dad about taking the ball. But I didn't tell Dad *who* took it. All the other kids were with me—they hate Bobby. Anyway, Dad saw Bobby on his own and told him he was in big trouble."

"Trouble for what?" asked his mom. "And who's Bobby?"

Sometimes his mother amazed him. Who's Bobby? As if she'd never heard of him before! "Aren't you listening?" he asked.

"I'm trying," she answered. "By the way, how did your father know about all this?"

"'Cause he's Santa," said Charlie matter-of-factly. Then he realized he was hungry. "What's for dinner?" he asked.

His mother's response totally baffled Charlie. "I'm going to kill Scott!" she announced.

Moms, he thought. Go figure.

If Charlie had known what was on his mother's mind, his good mood would have popped like a balloon. In fact, Laura was furious with Scott. He had obviously been telling Charlie even more crazy Santa Claus stories, even though he'd promised not to. Now Charlie was so confused he was having strange fantasies and turning violent!

She and Neal had to do something—and quickly.

❄   ❄   ❄

They were in court the very next morning. They would let a judge decide if Scott's craziness was harming Charlie. It was the only way.

But when the judge asked to speak with Charlie alone in his chambers, Laura began to worry. Maybe she and Neal shouldn't have brought the problem to court. After all, Scott did love Charlie a lot. She sighed.

"Do you really think we should go through with this?" she asked Neal. "Taking away Scott's visitation rights is awfully harsh."

"It's for the best," Neal told her. "Charlie's still talking about what happened last Christmas. That's not healthy or normal. He should be beyond the Santa Claus thing by now." He took Laura's hand. "I mean, come on, don't you remember when you stopped believing in Santa?"

"I do," said Laura softly. "I was around Charlie's age. I wrote Santa a letter every single week that year. All I wanted was a Mystery Date Game—remember those?— they don't even make them anymore.

"Well, anyway, Christmas came, and I got dozens of presents. Everything you can imagine. Everything but a Mystery Date Game. That's when I stopped believing."

"Exactly!" said Neal. "I was three when it happened. All I wanted was an Ovaltine Decoder Ring. But when Christmas came, no ring. That's when *I* stopped believing."

Laura stared at him. "You were *three*?"

At that moment Scott came bursting into the courtroom. His beard was full and snowy, and he wore a red sport jacket trimmed with white. He looked like Santa dressed for a cocktail party.

"Where's Charlie?" he demanded. "I want to talk to him."

"He's in with the judge," said Laura.

Just then Charlie and the judge came back into the courtroom. Charlie ran up to Scott.

"It's all okay, Dad," Charlie said to his father. "I told him everything."

Scott saw the expression on the judge's face. It was grim. That's what I was afraid of, he thought.

"My chambers," ordered the judge. Once Scott, Laura, and Neal were inside, he looked at Scott gravely. "Mr. Calvin," he announced, "I've reviewed everyone's testimony and come to a decision. I don't like to do this during the holidays, but in the best interest of the child I must. I am granting the petition of Dr. and Mrs. Miller. As of today, your visitation rights are suspended."

Scott had never felt so terrible in his life. How could they take his son away from him?

But they had. Slowly, Scott walked out of the courtroom to tell Charlie the news.

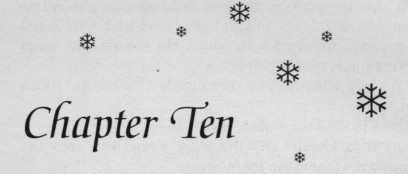

Chapter Ten

Scott was not giving thanks this Thanksgiving. He was crying.

He stood in the snow outside Neal and Laura's house, feeling miserable. He could see Charlie sitting at the dining table inside, and he looked miserable, too. He wasn't eating, just staring at the glass ball Bernard had given him. Scott sniffled. Life was terrible sometimes.

"Time to go." Without even looking down, Scott knew who it was. Bernard.

"I can't," he said.

"What's wrong?" asked the elf.

"I'm supposed to be Santa, right?"

"That's the general plan, yes," said Bernard.

"And being Santa means making children happy?" Scott shook his head. "How can I make other children happy when I've broken my own son's heart?"

Bernard looked up at him. "You've got two choices," he said. "You can stand out here feeling sorry for yourself, failing millions of kids and single-handedly killing off the

Christmas spirit. Or you can go into that house and deal with the problem—and then come with me."

For such a little man you are very smart, thought Scott. Then he headed for the front door.

❄   ❄   ❄

There was a turkey on the table big enough to feed Charlie's entire class, but only three places were set: for Charlie, for Neal, and for Laura. Charlie knew his mom had been cooking for days, and everything looked great, but he didn't have much of an appetite. He missed his dad.

His dad must have been missing him, too, because as soon as Charlie said grace—"Thank you for the food we are about to receive. Bless Mom, Neal . . . and bless Dad, too"—the doorbell rang.

And there was his father, right in their front hallway. Charlie was worried at first because Neal got angry with Scott for coming. He even tried to get him to leave, but Scott stopped him. Charlie had never seen his dad take charge like this—it was awesome!

Then Neal asked Scott if he still believed he was Santa.

"I don't know," said Scott.

Charlie was astonished. "What do you mean you don't know?" he asked his dad. "Of course you are! Think of all those kids—"

"The only kid I'm thinking about is you," said Scott.

"Dad, I'm fine," said Charlie. "But you can't let all those other kids down. They believe in you."

Neal whirled around. "Charlie, listen—," he began.

"No!" said Charlie. "YOU listen. You think you know him. You don't."

"Honey, you're confused," said Laura.

Charlie looked at her. "Mom," he said. "I know exactly who he is. He's Santa. We were at the North Pole together. I saw it. The elves are real old, even though they look like me. And reindeer can fly and smile. Right, Dad?"

Charlie tossed the glass ball to his father, who fumbled for it and caught it.

"Believing is seeing. Remember, Dad?" Charlie asked.

Believing is seeing? Judy the elf had said that, back at the North Pole, thought Scott. What was Charlie trying to tell him? Scott looked at the glass ball and saw that it was pulsing with light, glowing like some giant jewel. His eyes widened. He laughed. It *was* magic!

Laura and Neal stared at him blankly. Scott realized that they couldn't see that the ball was glowing. To them it was just a silly plastic toy.

He walked over to Charlie and kissed him on the cheek. "Could I just have a minute alone with my son?" he asked. "You know, to say good-bye properly?"

Neal and Laura nodded and said they'd wait in the dining room. When they were out of earshot, Charlie and Scott hugged. "Dad!" said Charlie. "You saw it, didn't you? You saw the ball come to life!"

"You bet I did," said Scott. "How'd you get it back?"

"Like you said—I had to believe. And it worked!" said Charlie. "It worked!"

Scott hugged Charlie again. "Look, Sport," he said. "Bernard's waiting for me. I've got to go."

"I'm coming, too, aren't I?" asked Charlie.

"I don't know," said Scott. He glanced in the direction of the dining room, where Laura and Neal waited. "Maybe you'd better stay here with your mom."

"Dad!" said Charlie. "I want to be with *you*."

"Oh, Sport," said Scott. "You don't know how many times I've wanted to hear you say that."

"So you mean I can go?"

Scott hesitated. Then a grumpy voice said, "So make up your mind, already!" It was Bernard.

Charlie was really glad to see him. "Can I go, Bernard?" he pleaded. "Please, can I go?"

"It's okay with me, Sport," said the elf. They turned to Scott, who threw up his hands with a grin. "How can I say no?" he asked.

And they were out of there.

Chapter Eleven

"It's nice to be back," said Scott. And it was. The weather at the Pole was clear and sunny. The elves were in high spirits. The production lines looked ready for the big Christmas push. And Judy's cocoa was even more delicious the second time around.

As he strolled toward the Workshop, Scott felt a surge of pride. The halls were lined with hundreds of photos and paintings of past Santas, and now he, Scott, was one of them. It was a great feeling.

"Soon I'll have my picture up there," he said to Bernard and Charlie. "I'm . . . I'm so honored."

But something was bothering Charlie. "Bernard?" he asked, looking up at the pictures. "How come there have been so many Santas?"

"That's . . . a good question," Bernard said slowly. "The best answer I can give you is . . . they suffer from professional burnout."

"You mean because the job is so demanding?" asked Scott.

"No," said Bernard. "I mean a lot of people keep fires

burning in their fireplaces, and some Santas . . ."

". . . suffer burnout." Scott finished the sentence with Bernard. He felt a little sick.

"Then there are overprotective homeowners." Bernard continued. "Santas get shot at. And, of course, quite a few Santas have gotten sucked into the exhaust of a DC-10. Oh, and storms are a real problem. . . ."

"Hey!" said Charlie. "Deal's off! No way! I'd rather have a live father than a dead—" He couldn't bring himself to finish. "Look, Bernard," he went on. "You're sending my dad out on a pretty dangerous mission. He'll need protection. You've got to bring this place into the twenty-first century. You need computers! Stealth technology!"

Bernard looked skeptical. "I don't know, Charlie," he said. "All that stuff sounds complicated. And expensive."

"I thought you said you guys were magical!" said Charlie indignantly.

"Magical!" scoffed the elf. "You think hot chocolate grows on trees? And you know what it costs to feed those reindeer? Comet eats like a horse!"

"Please, Bernard," Charlie pleaded.

The elf sighed. "I'll see what I can do."

❅   ❅   ❅

This sure beats the meetings at B and R, thought Scott as he was led into the Research and Development wing of Santa's Workshop the next day. Everyone was a lot more cheerful, for example. No yelling, no arguing, no table slamming. Just a lot of busy little elves, working hard to make life safe for him—the new Santa!

He found out quickly that they were doing a great job. Led by an elf called Quintin, and helped by Charlie, they'd come up with all kinds of amazing new safety devices. There was a Santa hat equipped with a two-way radio. There were radar-jamming jingle bells and a snow-screen attachment for the sleigh, which could now rise straight into the air like a rocket. As Quintin and Charlie showed him what they'd been doing, Scott found himself feeling better—and safer—every minute.

But it wasn't until he saw the modifications to his Santa costume that Scott began to get really excited. The new suit was a technical marvel. It looked fantastic, as if NASA, Calvin Klein, and Harley-Davidson had designed it together. It was fireproof and bulletproof, so Scott didn't have to worry about getting shot. Best of all, it came with special removable pom-poms. When thrown, the pom-poms released a nontoxic gas that soothed people and put them to sleep—instantly. They woke up happy, and with absolutely no memory of Santa.

"Use the pom-poms when someone spots you," Quintin told Scott. "When they wake up they'll think they were dreaming."

Scott beamed. He could hardly wait to take off.

❋   ❋   ❋

Back in his hometown, there were people who couldn't wait for Scott, either. There were the children, of course. But also Neal and Laura. And the police.

Neal and Laura were certain that Scott had visited

them on Thanksgiving to kidnap Charlie, and all they could think about was getting him back. They had gotten a phone call from Charlie, saying that he was safe—and then something about the North Pole and new technology. It only made them more convinced that their son was in the company of a madman. A dangerous madman. So they had been working closely with the police.

Neal had visited the station and talked to everyone there about Scott. "He'll come to us on Christmas Eve," he told them. "We've got to be ready."

So at the same time Scott and Charlie were taking off in the new attack-proof sleigh, a special heavily armed police squad was surrounding Neal and Laura's house.

And while Scott and Charlie enjoyed a cup of cocoa in the sky above the North Pole, the police were arresting every unfortunate person in the neighborhood who happened to be dressed up as Santa. They got seven in two hours. But none of them was Scott.

"He's not here," said Laura, who had been called to the station to see the Santa lineup. She fought back tears. Where *was* Charlie? This Christmas was a disaster.

❅   ❅   ❅

"This Christmas is the best," Charlie told Scott happily. Everything was perfect—the sleigh felt like an airborne Ferrari, the reindeer were acting like pussycats, and he was even helping his dad navigate. It was awesome.

Suddenly Charlie realized where they were. "Look, Dad," he said. "There's Mom and Neal's house! Let's go there next. I made something for them at the Workshop."

"Sure," said Scott. "I have something for them, too."

They headed down quickly, eager to leave their gifts under Neal and Laura's tree.

It turned out to be a big mistake.

The minute Scott got to the tree in the darkened living room, the lights came on and someone barked, "Freeze!" Then three policemen, guns drawn, closed in on Scott and handcuffed him. There was no time for him to throw a pom-pom, no way to call for help on his radio hat.

In spite of all his precautions, Santa Claus had been arrested.

Charlie, watching from the roof, was horrified. So were the neighborhood children. Attracted to their windows by the police sirens, they cried and shouted as Scott was forced into a patrol car. But their protests did no good. As Scott was driven away to the police station, a streetful of bewildered, sobbing children tried to make sense out of what they had witnessed. Santa arrested? How was it possible?

Back at the Pole, the elf named Larry burst into the control room. "We've got a problem," he said. "Santa was at the Miller's and he's not responding."

Quintin snapped to attention. "All right, Bernard, let's see how good your new security is," he said. Then he gave the order.

"Deploy E.L.F.S.!"

Instantly the crack rescue team that had been training for just this kind of emergency—four elves, dressed in jumpsuits, bristling with elf-size lethal weapons—strode out. They were E.L.F.S., the Effective Liberating Force

Squad, and they were as eager to attack as terriers sniffing out a rabbit. They linked arms, activated their jet packs, and flew off into the night.

Half an hour later they were on Charlie's roof, reporting for duty.

Their leader helped Charlie on with an official E.L.F.S. jacket. "Thanks," Charlie said solemnly, zipping it up. There was so much riding on this mission—the happiness of childrenkind! The future of Christmas! It was a big responsibility!

As his jet pack lifted him into the air, Charlie smiled. It was also an adventure he'd been waiting for all his life.

"Let's go save Santa!" he cried.

Chapter Twelve

Desk Sergeant Chuzzlewit didn't mind working on Christmas Eve. He liked a nice quiet shift, and absolutely nothing was happening at the station tonight. That was fine with him. It was restful.

Not a creature is stirring, he told himself with sleepy amusement. He yawned.

Then he heard a voice. He peered over the edge of his desk. A gang of little kids dressed in shiny jumpsuits and backpacks stood there staring up at him.

"We're looking for Santa Claus," said one.

"Go home, kids," said the sergeant. "Visiting hours are over."

"We're not kids. And we're not visiting," said another.

"We came here to bust out my dad," said a third. He was a little taller than the others, with larger features and a deeper voice. The sergeant peered at him. Had he seen that face before?

He checked the missing kid's photo on his desk. Yes!

"Hey!" he said, coming awake a little. "You're the Calvin kid! Who are your friends?"

"We are your worst nightmare," said one of them. "Elves with an attitude."

Before the sergeant could even wonder what the little fellow meant, the group had swarmed all over him, tied him up with ribbons, gagged him with a huge cone of cotton candy, and run off to the cells.

I was wrong, thought Sergeant Chuzzlewit as a huge chunk of cotton candy melted in his mouth. Creatures *are* stirring.

His friend Officer Charles found that out next. He was on duty near the holding cell when he heard a noise and ran in to investigate.

Officer Charles had been on the force for almost thirty years, so nothing much surprised him anymore. But when he saw four tiny men and a young boy in the cell with prisoner Calvin, his mouth fell open.

"What the . . . ?!" he began. Before he could finish they were all over him. In a matter of seconds his mouth was full of cotton candy and his arms and legs were immobilized, courtesy of many brightly colored ribbons.

And there was more. Officer Charles watched in amazement as one of the tiny men pulled some tinsel from the Christmas tree in the cell and began sawing the bars with it. He blinked with disbelief as the tinsel cut through the bars as if they were made of Play-Doh, not steel.

"Tinsel," said the E.L.F.S. leader. "It's not just for decoration."

The officer groaned in frustration as the entire party— Scott Calvin, the boy, and the four tiny men—cheered, ran out of the cell, and escaped into the night.

After wishing him a very merry Christmas, of course.

❋   ❋   ❋

As the E.L.F.S. headed back to the Pole, elated with the success of their mission, Scott and Charlie made their way to Neal and Laura's house. They had gifts to deliver, after all.

Neal answered the door. He looked overwhelmed with relief to see Charlie. "Thank heavens!" he cried, hugging him. "Are you all right?"

"I'm fine," said Charlie. He handed Neal the gift he'd made for him up at the Pole. "I just wanted to give you this."

A siren wailed in the distance. Police! Scott and Charlie looked at each other. "I don't have much time," said Scott as the siren drew closer.

"We can go now," Charlie told him. He was eager to get back to the sleigh. They had a lot more work to do tonight.

"No!" It was Laura, fighting back tears of relief now that she knew Charlie was safe. She hugged him as if she'd never let him go.

Charlie didn't want to hurt her feelings, but after a minute he had to pull away. He turned to his father as if to say, "Ready?"

Scott cleared his throat. "Ah . . . actually, Sport," he said, "I'm thinking that maybe it would be better . . . if . . . you stayed here with your mom."

Charlie couldn't believe his ears. Neither could Laura.

"What!" they exclaimed together.

"Dad!" said Charlie. "I want to be with *you*!"

"And I want to be with you," said Scott. "But I can't have you with me all the time—that would be too selfish, Son. How about if you stay here during the year, and next year, around Christmastime, we get together again?"

Now Charlie was fighting back tears. "I'll miss you too much!" he managed to say.

"I know." Scott's voice was very soft now. "But here's the thing—and this is a tough one." He knelt down so they were face-to-face.

"There are a lot—millions—of children who are counting on me. Who believe in me. I can't let them down, Sport. I have a lot of work to do."

Charlie knew what his father was trying to say. "So I can't be selfish, either," he finished for him. He knew his dad was right. But it was still hard getting the words out.

Scott gave Charlie a look full of love and tenderness. "Listen to me," Scott said. "You have given me a wonderful gift. You believed in me when no one else did. You helped make me Santa! Selfish? You're the least selfish person I know."

They hugged fiercely. "I love you, Santa," Charlie whispered in his father's ear.

"I love you, too," his father whispered back. Then he stood to face Laura.

"So what do you say, Laura?" he asked. "Charlie spends the year with you, but on Christmas Eve he comes with me. Is that all right?"

Laura looked at Scott. She had the uncanny feeling that

she was seeing him—really seeing him—for the very first time. She found herself grinning. "I can't believe it," she stammered. "It really *is* you. You're—Santa Claus!"

Scott's eyes twinkled. "It's something, isn't it?" he beamed.

A siren sounded again, much closer this time. Scott turned toward the door.

"Wait!" cried Laura. "Don't leave yet!" She ran into the study and returned seconds later carrying a thick legal document.

"This is my Christmas present to you," she told Scott. "The custody papers." And then she ripped them up.

Now it was Scott's turn to blink back a tear. "Thanks, Laura," he said. "Merry . . ." He couldn't finish.

"What's all this boo-hooin' about?" asked a familiar voice. It was Bernard, sounding as impatient and bossy as ever.

"Just saying good-bye," Scott told him, his voice husky.

"What good-bye?" demanded the elf.

"I'm not gonna see my dad for a long time," Charlie's voice was as sad as Scott's.

"You still got the glass ball?" Bernard asked him.

Charlie nodded yes.

"Just shake it whenever you want to be with your dad."

"Really?" Charlie's eyes widened. That changed everything!

Bernard raised an eyebrow. "Have I ever steered you wrong?"

Charlie grinned. They both knew the answer to that one.

Scott's takeoff in his sleigh was pretty spectacular. As the entire neighborhood watched, the reindeer leaped off the roof with the grace and precision of dancers. It was awe inspiring. Even the police, who had finally arrived at Neal and Laura's house, got misty-eyed.

Then Scott gave a mighty "HO, HO, HO!", the reindeer circled over Neal and Laura's house one last time, and three beautifully wrapped presents came down from the sky.

There was an Ovaltine Decoder Ring for Neal. The Mystery Date Game for Laura.

And a soccer ball for Charlie.

When he unwrapped it, Charlie missed his dad so badly that he panicked. How could he last a whole year without seeing his dad?

Then he remembered the glass ball.

He ran to his room and pulled it out of its hiding place in one of his soccer shoes. He carried it down to the back porch, shook it, and felt a thrill of joy as the ball began to pulse and glow with magical light.

He peered up at the sky hopefully. There were stars like crystal ornaments, and a bright crescent moon. That was all.

Charlie stood there, willing his father to appear. But he didn't. Fighting disappointment, Charlie headed for the back door.

"You miss me already? What's it been? Ten minutes? I mean, give me a break!" The voice was cranky. The voice was Scott's.

Charlie whirled around. There was his dad! As Charlie ran to him, Scott stopped pretending to be annoyed and opened his arms wide. "Want to go for a quick ride?" he asked.

"You bet!"

"Of course, it's up to your mother," said Scott. Laura was standing in the doorway watching them.

Charlie looked at her pleadingly. "Mom . . . ?"

"Get out of here, you two," she said.

So they did.